Table of Contents

Se

Unit 7 Re

Pausing Point (Stories for Assessment and Enrichment)

Core Knowledge Language Arts®

Seth
Unit 7 Reader

Skills Strand
KINDERGARTEN

Amplify learning.

Core Knowledge®

Seth

This is Seth Smith.

Seth is ten.

Se**th** must get in bed at ten.

Se**th** can jump on his bed, but not past ten.

Se**th** can stomp and romp and stand on his hands, but not past ten.

Seth's dad gets mad if
Seth is not in bed at ten.

Seth's Mom

This is Pat.

Pat is Se**th**'s mom.

Pat can fix **thing**s.

Pat can scrub, plan, and **th**ink.

Pat can run fast.

Pat can **sing** so**ng**s.

Seth's Dad

This is Ted.

Ted is Se**th**'s dad.

Ted is stro**ng**.

Ted can **ch**op big logs wi**th** his ax.

Ted can lift big stumps.

Ted can cru**sh** tin cans
wi**th** his hands.

Sal's Fish Shop

Pat and **Seth** went in Sal's Fi**sh Sh**op.

Sal had fre**sh** fi**sh**.

Sal had fre**sh** **sh**rimp.

Sal had crabs.

Sal had clams.

Sal had **squ**id.

Pat got fi**sh** and **sh**rimp.

Lunch

Seth had lunch with his mom and dad.

Pat had **sh**rimp and **ch**ips.

Ted had **sh**rimp, fi**sh**, and **ch**ips.

Seth had ham and **ch**ips.

Munch, munch.

Crunch, crunch.

Yum, yum.

Seth's Finch

That's Seth's pet fin**ch**, **Ch**ip.

Chip can flap his wi**ng**s.

Chip can mun**ch** on ants and bugs.

Chip can si**ng**.

Chip can land on Se**th**'s hand.

That fin**ch** is fun!

Lost Finch

Se**th**'s pet fin**ch**, **Ch**ip, is lost.

Se**th** can't spot him.

Pat can't spot him.

Ted can't spot him.

Chip is not on S**eth**'s bed.

Chip is not on S**eth**'s desk.

Then, at last, Pat spots **Ch**ip.

Chip hid in Pat's hat and slept.

Seth's Sled

Seth's sled went fast.

Seth held on.

Seth hit bumps but did not stop.

Seth hit slush but did not stop.

Then Seth's sled hit mud.

Spla**sh**!

Se**th** got mud on his sled.

Se**th** got mud on his pants.

Se**th** got mud on his hat.

Meg's Tots

This is Meg.

Meg is Pat's best pal.

Pat has 1 lad—Se**th**.

Meg has 5 tots—Tom, Tim, Max, Sam, and Wes.

Meg has **qu**ints!

Pat and Ted help Meg.

Pat sets Tim and Tom on Se**th**'s rug.

Ted sets Sam on Se**th**'s **qu**ilt.

Pat sets Max on Se**th**'s bed.

Ted helps Wes stand up on Se**th**'s desk.

Hash and Milk

Pat and Ted had lun**ch** wi**th** Meg's tots.

Max got ha**sh** on his **ch**in.

Wes got ha**sh** on his bib.

Tim's milk is on Tom.

Then Tom got milk on Tim.

Sam got milk on Pat and Ted.

About this Book

This book has been created for use by students learning to read with the Core Knowledge Reading Program. Readability levels are suitable for early readers. The book has also been carefully leveled in terms of its "code load," or the number of spellings used in the stories.

The English writing system is complex. It uses more than 200 spellings to stand for 40-odd sounds. Many sounds can be spelled several different ways, and many spellings can be pronounced several different ways. This book has been designed to make early reading experiences simpler and more productive by using a subset of the available spellings. It uses *only* spellings students have been taught to sound out as part of their phonics lessons, plus a handful of tricky words, which have also been deliberately introduced in the lessons. This means the stories will be 100% decodable if they are assigned at the proper time.

As the students move through the program, they learn new spellings and the "code load" in the decodable readers increases gradually. The code load graphic on this page indicates the number of spellings students are expected to know in order to read the first story of the book and the number of spellings students are expected to know in order to read the final stories in the book. The columns on the opposite page list the specific spellings and Tricky Words students are expected to recognize at the beginning of this reader. The bullets at the bottom of the opposite page identify spellings, tricky words, and other topics that are introduced gradually in the unit this reader accompanies.

Visit us on the web at www.coreknowledge.org

CORE KNOWLEDGE LANGUAGE ARTS

SERIES EDITOR-IN-CHIEF
E. D. Hirsch, Jr.

PRESIDENT
Linda Bevilacqua

EDITORIAL STAFF
Carolyn Gosse, Senior Editor - Preschool
Khara Turnbull, Materials Development Manager
Michelle L. Warner, Senior Editor - Listening & Learning

Mick Anderson
Robin Blackshire
Maggie Buchanan
Paula Coyner
Sue Fulton
Sara Hunt
Erin Kist
Robin Luecke
Rosie McCormick
Cynthia Peng
Liz Pettit
Ellen Sadler
Deborah Samley
Diane Auger Smith
Sarah Zelinke

DESIGN AND GRAPHICS STAFF
Scott Ritchie, Creative Director

Kim Berrall
Michael Donegan
Liza Greene
Matt Leech
Bridget Moriarty
Lauren Pack

CONSULTING PROJECT MANAGEMENT SERVICES
ScribeConcepts.com

ADDITIONAL CONSULTING SERVICES
Ang Blanchette
Dorrit Green
Carolyn Pinkerton

ACKNOWLEDGMENTS

These materials are the result of the work, advice, and encouragement of numerous individuals over many years. Some of those singled out here already know the depth of our gratitude; others may be surprised to find themselves thanked publicly for help they gave quietly and generously for the sake of the enterprise alone. To helpers named and unnamed we are deeply grateful.

CONTRIBUTORS TO EARLIER VERSIONS OF THESE MATERIALS
Susan B. Albaugh, Kazuko Ashizawa, Nancy Braier, Kathryn M. Cummings, Michelle De Groot, Diana Espinal, Mary E. Forbes, Michael L. Ford, Ted Hirsch, Danielle Knecht, James K. Lee, Diane Henry Leipzig, Martha G. Mack, Liana Mahoney, Isabel McLean, Steve Morrison, Juliane K. Munson, Elizabeth B. Rasmussen, Laura Tortorelli, Rachael L. Shaw, Sivan B. Sherman, Miriam E. Vidaver, Catherine S. Whittington, Jeannette A. Williams

We would like to extend special recognition to Program Directors Matthew Davis and Souzanne Wright who were instrumental to the early development of this program.

SCHOOLS
We are truly grateful to the teachers, students, and administrators of the following schools for their willingness to field test these materials and for their invaluable advice: Capitol View Elementary, Challenge Foundation Academy (IN), Community Academy Public Charter School, Lake Lure Classical Academy, Lepanto Elementary School, New Holland Core Knowledge Academy, Paramount School of Excellence, Pioneer Challenge Foundation Academy, New York City PS 26R (The Carteret School), PS 30X (Wilton School), PS 50X (Clara Barton School), PS 96Q, PS 102X (Joseph O. Loretan), PS 104Q (The Bays Water), PS 214K (Michael Friedsam), PS 223Q (Lyndon B. Johnson School), PS 308K (Clara Cardwell), PS 333Q (Goldie Maple Academy), Sequoyah Elementary School, South Shore Charter Public School, Spartanburg Charter School, Steed Elementary School, Thomas Jefferson Classical Academy, Three Oaks Elementary, West Manor Elementary.

And a special thanks to the CKLA Pilot Coordinators Anita Henderson, Yasmin Lugo-Hernandez, and Susan Smith, whose suggestions and day-to-day support to teachers using these materials in their classrooms was critical.

CREDITS

WRITERS

Matt Davis, Erin Kist, Juliane K. Munson, Rachel E. Wright

ILLUSTRATORS AND IMAGE SOURCES

All illustrations by Apryl Stott